OCEANSIDE PUBLIC LIBRARY
330 N COAST HWY
OCEANSIDE, CA 92054

ZOMBIE KID DIARIES™

GROSSERY GAMES

D1041284

Civic Center

GROSSERY GAMES

Writer - Fred Perry
Artist - Brian Denham
Inspiration & Concept - Brian Denham & Joe Dunn
Editors - Robby Bevard & Doug Dlin
Graphic Designer - Brian Denham
Cover Design - Brian Denham
Layout - Doug Dlin

Editor in Chief - Jochen Weltjens
President of Sales and Marketing - Lee Duhig
Art Direction - GURU-eFX
VP of Production - Wes Hartman
Publishing Manager - Robby Bevard
Publisher - Joe Dunn
Founder - Ben Dunn

Zombie Kid Diaries series
Zombie Kid Diaries 1: Playing Dead
Zombie Kid Diaries 2: Grossery Games
Coming Soon
Zombie Kid Diaries 3: Walking Dad

Also Available by the Author:
The Littlest Zombie Trade Paperback
PeeboManga 1.0

Come visit us online at
www.antarctic-press.com

Antarctic Press
7272 Wurzbach, Suite 204
San Antonio, TX 78240

Zombie Kid Diaries: Grossery Games, August 2012. *Zombie Kid Diaries* and all related characters are ™ and © Antarctic Press. Story © Fred Perry. Art © Brian Denham. No similarity to any actual character(s) and/or place(s) is intended, and any such similarity is purely coincidental. All rights reserved. Nothing from this book may be reproduced or transmitted without the express written consent of the authors, except for the purposes of review and promotion. *"But what Davros didn't count on was Cindy Lou Who and her Howling Commandos!"*

31232009734791

So, I started the first log book a while back to keep track of my daily high scores. It was supposed to give me an edge for my future as a pro gamer. But then I started writing other stuff too, like what the weather was like or how my day was. Eventually, my log book became more like a diary. Then I ran out of space and I had to get this new journal. Now I'm wondering if it's still worth keeping up with everything.

After all, my old plans were from before I became a zombie.

I guess I should keep this diary going, and consider it a chance to update my stats. Luckily, I remembered my old rubber stamp kit.

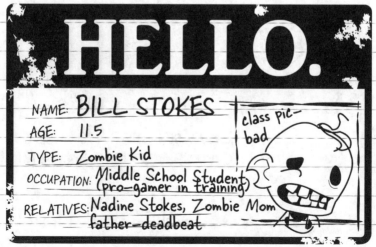

HELLO.

NAME: BILL STOKES
AGE: 11.5
TYPE: Zombie Kid
OCCUPATION: Middle School Student (pro-gamer in training)
RELATIVES: Nadine Stokes, Zombie Mom
        father-deadbeat

class pic-bad

I became a zombie when my mom brought home a virus from her medical test volunteer "job". She's a zombie too, though she's a bit more out of it than I am.

All in all, being a zombie isn't that different from being a regular kid. I just have to keep things looking normal—even when I have zits from beyond the grave, hair that defies any and all attempts at brushing or combing, and dangerous gas or bad breath stinky enough to drop a full-grown bull elephant, or at least Mr. Whipple's doberman, from ten feet away!

Q: HOW DO YOU STOP A CHARGING ELEPHANT AND A CHARGING GUARD DOG?

A: TAKE AWAY THEIR CHARGE CARDS! SO THEY CAN'T BUY GAS MASKS!

I once grew a mustache. A real mustache! I looked

like a truck driver or a crime lord! I couldn't wait
to show it off on Monday! I thought for sure that
nobody was going to mess with me from then on!

Unfortunately, almost all of my mustache hair fell out
right onto the pillow by Monday morning, leaving me
with just a little stubble that didn't make it past my
shower. The one time that zombie virus was going to
pay off for me, and it was a false alarm!

Being turned into a zombie kid changed the rules of the game on me, but not all of the changes were bad! For one, I discovered that I can stare without blinking for an incredibly long amount of time. That lets me keep focused on a video game screen for far longer than any normal kid.

Then there's the matter of a zombie's superior reflexes! No normal human can ever get the jump on a zombie while turning a blind corner. Once again, the advantages for an up-and-coming pro-gamer in training, like me, are tremendous!

I wanted to explain all that so I could talk about how Mom got her new job at Mal-Mart. Being zombies leads to some of our stuff wearing out a little faster than expected, like our Tupperware, so we have to restock on basics occasionally.

TUPPERWARE LOCKS IN FRESHNESS, BUT MOM'S CHOCOLATE MOUSE SOUFFLE STAGED A JAILBREAK!

I went along to check out the video games and score some underpriced memory sticks, since I sell save-games on iBay. Not everyone has time to clear all levels, bonuses and maps for their hard-mode role-playing video games.

A shifty-looking punk in a long overcoat was rushing out of the store just as we were leaving. He went right on through those crook detectors and set off every alarm in the building! That overcoat must have been full of loot!

He selected just the right time to make his move, too. The cashiers were changing shifts, and security were keeping their eyes on the cash boxes instead of on anyone trying to rip them off. Mr. Shifty was on his way out and would have gotten clean away...if not for Mom.

It was like watching one of those nature documentaries, and for me, it was all in slow motion. Mom tackled that guy like a cobra striking a mouse that never even saw it coming!

I understand why Mom just pounced like that. I probably would've tackled that guy myself if I'd been closer than she was. Someone who has that much in common with a turkey sandwich shouldn't just dart around like that! Lucky for him, we had a big dinner before leaving for the store. Lucky for us, Mom's and my zombieness is still a secret.

These days, it seems harder to distinguish what's going on around me when I'm not looking directly at it. I can't rely on my other senses that much either, because everything smells different now.

People smell like pastries or burgers. If I'm not looking right at a guy, it seems like some chocolate cake is talking on a cell phone right next to me!

As soon as Mom noticed he wasn't a toasted submarine sandwich flying through the Mal-Mart exit, she stopped, but she'd already knocked the daylights out of him with that lightning-fast tackle. The shoplifter didn't wake up until the store security and the cops got there.

The store manager came out to give Mom a pat on the back, and on the spot offered her a job as a Mal-Mart greeter and shoplifter-tackler! So that's how Mom got her new job. I wonder how long that'll last?

So, that's pretty much the zombie life situation at the moment. I guess I'll keep on writing this diary. It helps to keep track of daily events that might have affected my scores. In spite of being a zombie, I still want to be a professional gamer! One day, these diaries will be the statistical edge I need to make me the grand champion in the world of video game e-sports! An arena should fully emerge right about the time I'm ready to take the spotlight!

Super Smasher Sisters: 54 wins, 32 perfects.
(Avoided my team members today to let them rack up some points from online scrub victims. I'm so nice.)

Call of Honor 7: 67 victories, 21 blast streaks.

P.S.: Four scrubs rage-quit during my last Call of Honor blast streak! That reduced my overall score, but the salt from those virtual teardrops were scrum-dilly-icious!!

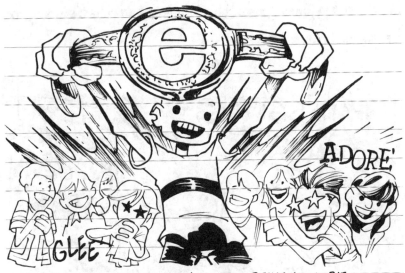

NOTHING CAN STOP ME! EXCEPT BEING A ZOMBIE. AND MIDDLE SCHOOL. THAT'S THE HITCH.

<u>Wednesday</u>

Sunny in the morning. Partly cloudy near the evening.

The annual "Spanksgiving Day Spectacular" fighting game tournament is starting next Friday, and I need to get warmed up to win that cash prize! Five hundred big ones go to the winner, and that's going to be yours truly!

At first, I was just interested in this contest as a good way to practice up and maybe earn a little spending cash on the side. But then I heard Mago Umehara, the Japanese gamer champ, was coming to town to visit relatives. He talked about his trip in an interview on *Gamebleat*'s site, and what he said kind of burned me up!

Mago said, "I am honored to be invited to that tournament, and I am hoping to encounter some talented competitors there who will try their best to defeat me. The American contestants look confident, but I will be the winner."

Translation: "I'm the baddest in the world, and no one can stop me, especially in this small backwater town, but those scrubs are invited to try!" Hey, I can read between the lines! I know smack talk when I read it!

I have got to take this guy down! Nobody comes to my home town and enters one of my local tournaments with that kind of veiled smack talk and gets away with it!

TRANSLATION: "THOSE SUCKERS WON'T EVEN SEE IT COMING."

TRANSLATION: "I'M GONNA STYLE ON ALL THEM FOOLZ."

Plus, when everyone sees that our tournament players can put the champ in his place, our town will become the new mecca of pro gaming! Folks will come from everywhere to learn and compete, and I'll finally get the respect and recognition I deserve from a thriving gamer community!

"MR. BILL STOKES—I MEAN, KID DRACULA? HOW DO YOU FEEL ABOUT THE TWENTY-BILLION-DOLLAR SPONSORSHIP OFFER FROM MEGAGAMES?"

"FRANKLY, I'M JUST GLAD THE PRO-GAMER SCENE HAS FINALLY FOUND ITS FOOTING IN THE MEDIA. BUT THE MILLIONS IN SPONSORSHIP DEALS SURE ARE A PLEASANT BONUS!"

Upholding the honor of our local gaming community would be a guaranteed slam dunk if not for one detail: I have to find a new, tougher controller to use.

This afternoon, I accidentally sliced open my controller's "A" button and realized that darned virus mutation isn't finished with my life yet.

I now have zombie claws. This didn't happen overnight, but gradually, or I would've noticed before ruining my controller.

I wonder how long I'll keep having these unexpected mutation side effects. I never seem to get anything cool like gigantic muscles, x-ray vision, or suddenly having bat wings sprout from my back.

Art by Bill Stokes.
Original art by Jenny Fong.
I traced this from Page 15 panel 3
Mega Max Volume 12 #76 June issue

Maybe if I just play carefully, these claws won't get in my way. Like when I'm careful while holding a pen. Either that, or find a way to cut my bone-hard, razor-sharp fingernails!

The broken controller kept me from my gaming for the night, so I just chucked it into one of my side pouch carry-alls and went downstairs into the bathroom to find the nail clippers. When I found them, they were warped at the handle, dulled and contorted beyond use. It was like someone used them to cut through a bale of barbed wire! Before I could put two and two together, Mom came home and saw me standing there trying to figure out what had mangled the nail clippers.

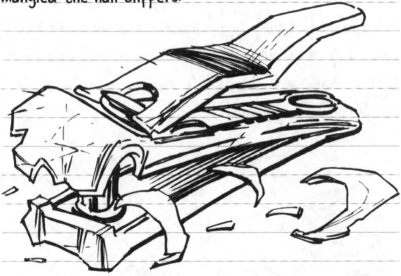

The next thing I knew, she grabbed my hands, looked at them, and then gave a disapproving zombie-mom grunt and shook her head! Like I was a four-year-

old who couldn't figure out how to groom himself!
Mom chucked the clippers in the wastebasket, then—
and I'm not even making this up—she gnawed off my
finger claws with her teeth! Zombie moms don't gnaw
like normal moms! It was like getting a manicure from
a lawnmower!

(A REAL NAIL-BITER)

Weird as that was, my fingernails were neat, clean and
back to normal after just twenty seconds of being
in Mom's wood-chipper mouth! I bet she figured out
how to do that after she broke the clippers. I was
so amazed with how neat everything turned out, I

hardly cared when Mom chewed up and swallowed the clippings! I should have known what was coming next, though, especially after she had me sit down in the chair.

As soon as she started pulling my shoes and socks off, I figured it out. I literally had to put my foot down! No way I was letting her give me a zombie-mom pedicure! She would not back off until I promised to keep my toenails trimmed myself.

Still...my nails do kind of taste like stale granola. The opportunity for a light snack could be why she was anxious to trim them. Once again, I wonder if Mom's trying to still be Mom, or if she's on some kind of zombie-mom autopilot.

I was so put off by that whole ordeal that I almost forgot to get back to practice with Super Smasher Sisters, the featured fighting game of the upcoming Thanksgiving tournament. With my "claws" trimmed, I was right back in form, setting traps, punishing impatience or just getting in that first surprise strike with my mutated reflexes. Even using an older, spare controller! When I'm in the zone, I'm unstoppable! So just you wait, Mr. Japanese Fighting Game Champion! Billzilla's in town!

Super Smasher Sisters: 80 wins, 56 perfects. (Fought Larry and Janine! They both lost bad, but they're gettin' better!)

Call of Honor 7: 12 victories, 8 blast streaks. (Cut back on my CoH practice to prepare for the tournament.)

P.S.: One guy sent me a text that said all my wins against him were luck. Hey, buddy, I don't wear green! I don't have a clover!

<u>Thursday</u>
Partly Cloudy.

Man, I was in such a good mood yesterday! The chance to defend my local gaming community's honor this weekend was the best news I had all month! Then my homeroom teacher had to rain on the parade. Mrs. Crabtree showed up to class today, wearing a Pilgrim outfit.

Mrs. Crabtree had dressed up to give us the "good news": a class field trip to "Camp Woodchunk" for Thanksgiving weekend. A huge, five-day authentic Pilgrim and Native American Thanksgiving feast.

That was enough to get the whole class excited.
Even my best friends Larry and Janine were pumped!
Larry is normally a quiet, geeky sort of guy, and
Janine is a girl obsessed with cute things. They both
play the same games I do, and they make decent

enough rivals and teammates. But there they were, excited about the trip! Didn't they know our reputation was at stake during the big tournament that weekend?

There's a catch, though. There's always a catch! In order to pay for the field trip, we have to sell boxes of frosted Thanksgiving cookies. Mrs. Crabtree had a sample box on her desk, and she passed out order forms to the whole class.

During lunch, I sat Larry and Janine down to talk about the "Spanksgiving Day" tourney. I thought if I explained how the champ was coming to squash our dignity, I could snap them out of this field trip nonsense, but no. Their brains were completely taken in! The whole class had been changed into field trip zombies, and I was the only sane thinker in the bunch!

Everyone started talking about how many cookies they would sell. It looks like the whole class has to make a quota for the trip to become a reality...which means that anyone slacking off is going to take a bunch of heat.

At least, that's how Mrs. Crabtree was pushing this thing. As if everybody who failed to sell their quota of cookies would be seated in the front row where the other kids could throw erasers or shoot rubber bands at the backs of their heads! I guess I'll have to go along with it this time, going door to door selling cookies, just to keep off everyone's hate-radar.

After I got home from school, I went over to Janine's for our Thursday night practice rounds. By that time, both she and Larry had a chance to check out that interview and see for themselves how Mago Umehara was calling us all out. They don't read between the lines as well as I do, it seems. They said I was getting a little paranoid and that this trip might be a good chance for me to relax. Horse pickles, I say!

So I went home a little bit early and started writing in here to let off some steam. I'm still stressed over this, though. Yesterday's news made my month, but this whole Thanksgiving field trip situation could ruin my life!

Super Smasher Sisters (offline): 16 wins, 8 perfects.

Friday
Mostly Sunny.

Aw, man. For the past few days, I forgot to put down what I have been eating. That's a pretty big error on my part, because that's the whole point of this journal: to be a log of all the important information from here on so it can be processed by some future computer program down the road.

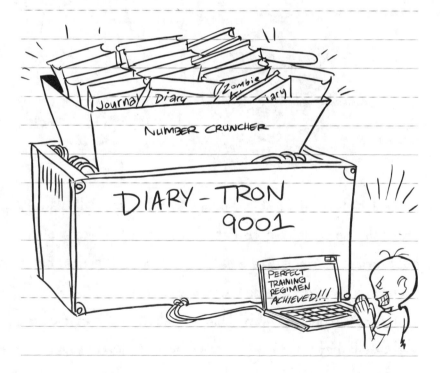

The weather, what I ate for breakfast, and how my day went will all be factors for analysis. All that information, dating back to middle school, will help that program give me the conditions for my optimum gaming performance when I'm a big-time veteran pro-gamer!

Since I became a zombie, normal food tastes all bland and ashy now. I have to eat stuff that'll make a billy goat gruff! Meals like meat lover's street pizza, or squirrel wings, or blended worm smoothies. Stuff that grosses me out just thinking about it, but tastes and smells better than the best waffle house super Sunday flapjacks ever...back when I liked flapjacks.

RUTTI TUTTI, GROSS AND FRUITY

i Can Be Flapjackz?

FLIP

FLIP O' WRIST ACTION

This morning, my mom just warmed up the cockroach cluster leftovers from yesterday morning in the microwave. I love it when they pop in there! We were sitting down and eating when I noticed she had on her Mal-Mart shirt with an "Employee of the Week" tag.

EMPLOYEE OF THE WEEK

☆ BEAUTIFUL JOB ☆

Surprised, I asked her, "Wow, Mom! How many shoplifters did you tackle in the last few days?" She tried to say it, but it just came out as "Hnnnhks." So she horse-stomped her right foot six times.

It was at breakfast that I came up with a brilliant plan. The answer to the Thanksgiving field trip and the cookie-selling business in one solution!

I'd just go ask Mom to deal with it, while I washed my hands of the whole thing! I gave her my order form and asked her to take it to work and get her co-workers to fill out the orders. Even before she became a zombie, my mom couldn't sell a dollar for fifty cents, never mind cookies to disgruntled Mal-Mart clerks!

Maybe I should feel a little guilty for handing this off, but every other kid in the world is going to do this too. The difference is, with my mom, I'm GUARANTEED to make zero sales, and that's awesome! This entire field trip fundraiser is sure to fail because of the lack of funds, but it won't be my fault at all, because nobody bought any cookies from my mom at work! I'm in the clear!

So now, nothing can stop me! I'm coming for you, Mr. Mago Umehara! You're in for the surprise of a lifetime if you think you can romp and stomp your way to victory in MY neck of the woods!

But the rest of the day didn't go so well. At lunch, the topic nobody could get over was the stupid field trip. I pretended to be just as excited, just to blend in and keep from drawing unnecessary attention to myself. Keeping a low profile is even more crucial for me now! The absolute worst-case scenario for me involves getting noticed!

"LOOK OVER THERE! THAT KID IS PURPOSELY GETTING MEDIOCRE GRADES TO KEEP OUT OF ADVANCE PLACEMENT COURSES, SO HE CAN BUCK THE SYSTEM TO BECOME A LEGENDARY PRO-GAMER LEGEND!"

"OH, AND LOOK AT HIM TRYING TO SABOTAGE THE FIELD TRIP SO HE CAN SNEAK OFF TO SOME BIG GAME TOURNAMENT! WE CAN'T HAVE THAT, NOW, CAN WE?"

"AND DOESN'T HE LOOK A BIT ZOMBIE-LIKE LATELY? LET'S CALL THE *FBI PARANORMAL FILES* GUYS ON HIM!!!"

Getting noticed is the very LAST thing I want to happen to me. But there's a problem with being in chameleon mode. Sometimes being part of the herd means you have to deal with predators just like everybody else. Last Halloween, our resident bully Steve put on a prank show and aired it during an assembly.

Steve's thing was a rip-off of some stupid reality TV game show called *Gross-eries*. It was basically videotaped bullying, but our idiot vice-principal, Mr. Horshack, loved it and wanted Steve to make monthly episodes! He even put Steve and his clique in charge of the school's audiovisual aids!

I was there just blending in, when Steve and his crew rolled through the cafeteria, looking for victims to bully on camera. Usually I pretend to eat, have my chat with Larry and Janine, then get out of there before Steve finishes his lunch. But I stayed a little too long this time. I was trying to make my interest in that useless field trip seem genuine, and I lost track of Steve's progress. Steve made a bee-line for me, and just like that, I was the next contestant on his stupid reality game show!

Steve doesn't like me all that much. Just this fall, we've had eight or nine bully-victim run-ins. And he's really had it out for me ever since he and his big brother ganged up on me out on the school's track field. They beat me up pretty badly, but I got my licks in...or rather, I got my bites in!

Not to mention the lunch period on the day before that, when Steve tried to kick me in the face!

I caught his ankle right in my teeth. He tasted like a strawberry Gushbomb candy! Because of that, Steve keeps his distance from my face, but he's still a jerk to me.

So there I was, trapped in front of the school's official A/V camera with Steve as the game show host. In his fist were some quiz questions for me to answer. If I got two out of the three right, I won, but if I failed, I had to "get gross". The "gross" in this quiz was that the loser had to swallow one fried dung beetle for every wrong answer.

Ha! If he only knew what my diet was like! I almost thanked him for bringing me some snacks, but I had to keep cool and pretend I was grossed out. Actually, those dung beetles smelled really good!

The quiz questions he asked were from Mr. Washington's last geometry test, the one I had to work hard NOT to get an "A++" in. Looking back on it, I should have just answered correctly, so he could move on to someone else, but I wanted a snack! So, I drew things out and made it look like I was struggling with finding the answer, the way they do on those "Weak Link"—style game shows.

I tried to act intimidated, but Steve didn't quite buy
it. I got two out of three wrong and tried to make
eating those delicious dung beetles look as distasteful
as possible. Two of the other kids got grossed
out watching and ran to the trash can to spew.
Everybody was convinced I was sincerely the loser
except Steve. Seeing me down that beetle must have
reminded him of the time I ate Larry's "fake worm"
in biology class last month.

The class bell rang, so that was that, but Steve was
hardly satisfied. He grinned menacingly, "Don't worry,

Bill, you'll have plenty of extra chances to answer questions now that you're a regular on my show!'"

So that's why today was not all good news. The upside was the snack! Man, those were good! I wish I'd had something that tasted that good when I was a regular kid! And you can buy bugs off the shelf at pet stores! I have to get Mom to go grocery shopping there!

Super Smasher Sisters: 57 wins, 31 perfects.

<u>Sunday</u>

Sunny all day.

Mealworms (Got Mom to pick up some from the pet store. Didn't have to ask her twice!)

Saturday was pretty uneventful. I just stayed home and practiced games all day. I was in top form all day, but yet again, Larry and Janine weren't online for practice! I need a chat with those two!

On Sundays I usually just hang out and watch online videos of matches—no practice or competitive gaming. But today was different. Today there was a live stream of Mr. Mago Umehara playing online—and he was playing nearby! He is already in town! After

45

seeing that, I just had to sign in and hunt him down. I wanted to give him a preview of the town-pride butt-whipping I am going to hand him at the tournament this coming Friday!

I found him pretty quickly. He was giving the local scrubs a righteous beat-down in a free-play room that anyone could join. Rather than use my main kick-butt user tag of "Kid Dracula," I decided to use one of my alternate gamer tags and join in with a character I don't use that often: "Kittychu", Janine's annoyingly cute main character. Yes, I wanted complete humiliation for this, and I wanted to do it anonymously!

I have to admit, he was good at adapting to my basic strategies. He won the first round we played, but just barely. Little did he know I was just messing around! For rounds two and three, he got the full-on zombie-kid assault! I'm talking total and complete ownage!

All I needed to do was wait for an opening or a mistake and use my mutated reflexes to get the jump on him! That test sealed the deal for me too. It is going to be a black Friday for the champ! Kid Dracula is our town's best and last defense!

I offered the champ a rematch, but he had to sign off. Yeah, sure! He just did not want to lose anymore! I was all set to serve him a nice, cold double shot of "P" on the rocks. "P" for "Perfect Defeat"! But it was satisfying enough to see the champ run for cover, so I just signed off after handing out a few more butt-kickings. I can't wait until Friday! Mr. Mago Umehara is going to eat every word of smack talk he said in that interview!

Super Smasher Sisters: 8 wins 6 perfects.

READY! TO GET SERVED, CHAMP?

TALL MUG ICE COLD PERFECT DEFEAT PERFECT DEFEAT

IT'S ON THE HOUSE!

<u>Monday</u>
Rainy all day long.
More mealworms, sauteed in garbage gravy

I knew things were going too smoothly. I was all
set for breakfast and totally hyped for Friday,
then, right out of the blue, Mom handed me some
paperwork. It was a permission slip and a completely
filled—out order sheet for the field trip! A whole
sheet full of orders, and checks to cover them all!
Just like that, I was hosed! I still don't believe this!

Somehow, my mom, who can barely speak one—
syllable sentences now, managed to sell a boatload of

Thanksgiving cookies to her co-workers at Mal-Mart!
How did she pull that off!?!

At school I found out what happened, and why Janine
and Larry have been so absent from online practice.
The whole truth came out at lunch when they were
discussing how successful their weekend fund-raiser
kiosk worked out!

Get this: Janine and Larry got their parents to
set up a little sales stand in front of Mal-Mart to
take orders for cookies. And my mom helped them
get permission from the store manager to do it! No
wonder Janine and Larry were too busy to practice

with me online! I've got traitors attacking my plans
from every conceivable angle!

To top it all off, Janine and Larry were both
expecting me to be grateful that they helped me meet
my quota. Janine smiled innocently. "We knew you'd
be too busy obsessing on practice to focus on this,
Bill."

Larry agreed. "Yeah, and we knew you'd be too proud
to ask for help, so we lent you a hand anyway! Now
we can all have a blast this weekend!" UGH! They
ruined everything!

That's not all that went wrong today. Vice-Principal
Horshack was paying another visit to the cafeteria
during lunch with his new best buddy, Steve! I can't
believe the pull that Steve has now that his stupid
game show is running! It's like the vice-principal is
convinced that Gross-eries is going to make the school
famous. That was when Janine let me know that
Steve's got permission to film segments on his show
during the field trip! I felt like I was in quicksand!
All my hopes and dreams were crashing down all around
me, and there was nothing I could do about it.

When I got home, I didn't even want to practice. I didn't touch the controller or boot up the game console. I just sat in my chair and started writing. I felt numb, defeated and hopeless. That's where I am right now: I just don't care anymore. I try as hard as I can to make something of myself. I give it my absolute best to work myself into something the world can get behind, the greatest pro-gamer ever, defend our nation's honor, and all I get is unlimited grief!

Am I reaching too high? Am I over-achieving? Why does fate have it in for me? Why?

Tuesday
Still rainy.

Guess what? I have a glimmer of hope! There's a chance I can skip out on the field trip! Here's the deal: Mrs. Jefferson was out walking her yappy little poodle again this morning, and Froufrou was barking at every stupid thing that moved, including me at the bus stop.

I cannot stand that dog, especially because she smells like pastry now! There's nothing worse than an eclair with a snooty, yappy attitude!

Mrs. Jefferson came up and picked up Froufrou, who licked all over her face. I guess Froufrou likes the taste of heavy, HEAVY make-up. It seems Mrs. Jefferson had it in her head that Froufrou likes me, because she wanted me to babysit her poodle while she's away on a trip this weekend with her best friend, Mrs. Horshack.

At first, I wanted to decline, but then I realized what she had just said. I asked, "Wait a minute... you're friends with Mrs. Horshack? Vice-Principal Horshack's wife?" When Mrs. Jefferson said yes, I knew right then and there that if I played my cards right, I could pull off the deal of the

century! Froufrou is going to help me make it to the tournament!

I agreed to help Mrs. Jefferson out and watch Froufrou, but then I pretended to suddenly remember the field trip. I said I would need help explaining to my teacher that I couldn't go and had to watch Froufrou, "my favorite poodle in the whole wide world!" Mrs. Jefferson bought that whole story, hook, line and sinker!

She's going to talk to Mr. and Mrs. Horshack and arrange something so that Froufrou and I can be

together this weekend, because we're such good pals!
Slam dunk! Home run! SCORE! I don't have to go on
that FIELD TRIP!!! I even tried to kiss Froufrou in
gratitude, but that darned dog bit my nose!

So here's my plan: As soon as Mrs. Jefferson takes
off for her trip, I'll tie Froufrou in the back yard,
leave some dog food, and let her cool her heels
until Monday when Mrs. Jefferson returns. Once
Froufrou's on lockdown, I'll take the city bus to the
mall Friday afternoon and roll back home in the limo
they'll undoubtedly provide for the tournament's big
winner! This plan is so full of win, it can't possibly
fail.

Today would have gone off without a hitch if not for Steve and his camera crew. Yup, they were shooting another episode of Gross-eries in the cafeteria. This time, they were messing with big Harold, a.k.a. "Death Butt"! They were asking him questions from Social Studies class, and this time, the penalty for getting two out of three questions wrong was a handful of crickets. I had no idea why the teachers let Steve get away with that until Janine clued me in.

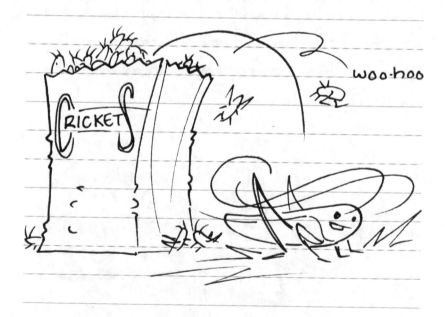

woo-hoo

CRICKET

Janine frowned as she told me why Steve was allowed to do this. "He's been looking up 'edible insects' ever since Mr. Barbarino's biology class brought up the subject. He has an entire book on *Bugs that People Can Eat and How to Prepare Them.* I'm not happy about it—last week, he made me eat a scorpion and filmed the whole thing!"

It was kind of weird, seeing always-happy, cutesy Janine upset about something. According to her, Mr. Barbarino's cleared all of Steve's "Gross-eries penalties" as actual healthy, educational snacks! That means the school staff is actually backing up Steve's shenanigans. This has got to be some kind of a joke!

Harold wasn't having it, though. He just flat-out refused to eat those crickets after he got the questions wrong. Good for him! But then, Steve, Mr. Picky Eater himself, got upset and yelled, "They taste like chocolate-covered peanuts, dummy! Look!"

Then Steve grabbed a honkin' handful of squirming crickets, took a big, cake-eating bite out of the cluster, and started eating them! Steve didn't stop until his hand was empty. He even licked his chops after downing that whole batch!

That was enough for Harold, though. He went straight for the nearest trashcan and spewed, which started a chain reaction that grossed out at least five other kids! At that point, I could hear Vice-

Principal Horshack's weirdo laugh from across the cafeteria. He was watching the whole thing and loving it! I'm guessing the Vice-Principal is just interested in seeing the school's version of his favorite show kick it up a notch, but I don't know what got into Steve! Last month, he was grossed out if anyone sneezed near his food!

Super Smasher Sisters: 44 wins, 31 perfects. (In top form tonight.)

Wednesday
Sunny or partly cloudy.
Leftover Roadkill Casserole. Mom's getting fancy.

Someone up there hates me! Someone up there thinks
my life should be like a yo-yo and is just yanking
my chain up and down! Today, I got called to the
office to see Vice-Principal Horshack for a special
conference about the field trip we're about to
take. At first, I was excited: "Right on cue! Give
me my free pass out of this mess, please!" I was all
packed up and ready to go just like everybody else,
just to make my disappointment look that much more
convincing.

While I was waiting to talk to Mr. Horshack, Mrs.
Jefferson came in...with Froufrou! Mrs. Jefferson
was dressed in outdoorsy clothes, hiking boots, and
had a knapsack. Froufrou had on a doggie version of
Mrs. Jefferson's hiking jacket, plus little doggie hiking
boots on her feet. That was all I needed to see to
get it.

Mrs. Jefferson had changed her vacation plans! She
and Froufrou were coming with the class! That
quicksand feeling was starting to seep in again...but
that was just the beginning. Mr. Horshack had called
me in to give me the official title of "Trip Mascot

Caretaker!" It was going to be my job to look after Froufrou for the next FIVE DAYS!

There went my weekend! There went my shot at the champ! There went the honor and dignity of our local gaming scene! I wanted to scream at the top of my lungs right then and there! But all I could do was stare into infinity.

The hurting didn't end there—that was just the beginning! As we boarded the field trip bus, I was a little too slow, since my feet feel like they're made of lead when I try to run.

It's a major down side of being a zombie: lightning—quick reflexes, slow as heck after leaving the starting block. So I was the last kid on the last bus. And who did I have the pleasure of sharing a seat with? You guessed it, the host of Gross-eries, good old Steve! Steve isn't even in our class! How did he get invited!? Oh, yeah—of course Vice-Principal Horshack's best pal gets to come. He probably didn't even need to pay, thanks to Mom's cookie kiosk sales!

For twenty minutes, I had to endure "accidental" elbows to my ribs, "friendly" jabs to the arm, kicks that weren't REALLY kicks, and the occasional stomp on the toe. Easily, this was the single worst day of my entire life!

After a while, I'd had enough. I was going to block, dodge or counter any "accidental" attack from that point on. And I did! I dodged three times straight. But the strange thing was, it was hard! Steve's reflexes were good...scary good.

And after the third miss, Steve just shrugged it off and said, "Whatever. I'll get you when you ain't lookin'."

"So I'm always going to be looking," I said. Then I just stared at him! I didn't blink or anything! That started an impromptu staring contest. Yeah! I got

him to play MY mind games for a change! No human could possibly hope to out-stare a zombie! Even so, he would have probably won if I were still a normal kid. It took him at least five whole minutes to blink, and that's really good!

I guess that staring contest made me lose track of the time and where we were, because I almost missed that we passed right by Woodcreek Mall, the same mall that's hosting the big tournament this coming Friday! It was like someone up there wasn't satisfied with me losing the opportunity of a lifetime. Now I was being teased with the fact that I was being held in a Thanksgiving prison camp just four miles away from—

Wait a minute.

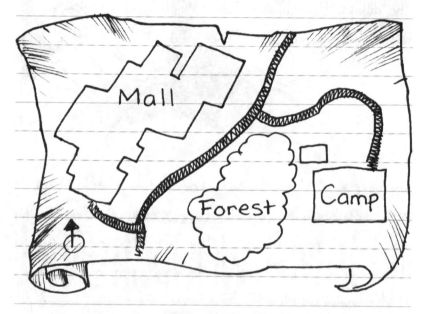

It's just four miles away! I could hike that! All I need to do is slip away real quiet-like on Friday afternoon. The tournament only has sixteen slots. It would barely take two hours! Yeah, I'll be back before anyone knows I was gone! The only hang-up is the fastest I can hike these days is a slow shuffle, but at least there's hope! I have a shot at this again! I just need a plan...an ESCAPE plan!

I wish I'd thought of all that when I got off the bus
at the campsite, because my attitude would have been
a little less dreary and I could've kept my eyes open
for stuff to help with my big escape. I was down in
the dumps, though, and Camp Woodchunk's scenery
wasn't helping matters.

Camp Woodchunk isn't a real get—back—to—nature
camping ground. The whole place is like a stripped—
down amusement area and outdoor barbecue diner.
It's as if someone was trying to make a great
Jurassic—era theme park but just had chipmunks and
raccoons to work with.

The camp counselors were all waiting for us when we got off the bus to help us unload our bags and take them to the barracks. They were all dressed in Pilgrim or Native American outfits, and they looked sappy. With fake smiles and forced cheer all over the place, none of them really looked like they wanted to be there. That made me feel a little less lonely in my misery.

The one person working there who DID look genuinely happy to see everybody was this guy calling himself "Miles Standish". Under my breath, I muttered, "Get a load of THIS poser." Janine and Larry heard me and they laughed. Unfortunately, Mr. Horshack heard me too and made me shush up, and Steve agreed with him. UGH! Do I hate those two! A bully with the vice-principal for a "best buddy" is the worst kind of bully I can possibly imagine!

THUMBS UP FOR EVIL!

Mr. Standish was there to welcome us to his "Pilgrim Camp" this Thanksgiving and to explain the rules, and he did it in the worst Old English accent I've ever heard. You could just tell that this guy was from the South Bronx portion of Jolly Old England! No one really knew what he meant when he kept asking "Know what I mean?" every ten to twenty seconds.

"BADABINGETH! LET'S GETTETH DIS
T'ANKSGIVIN' T'ING STARTED OVER HERE!"

The boys and girls got to stay across from each other in different barracks. Breakfast, lunch and Thanksgiving dinner were going to be served every day at appointed times. Blah, blah, blah. The gateways

(prison guard posts) were manned by counselors, and you could only go through if a counselor or teacher was with you.

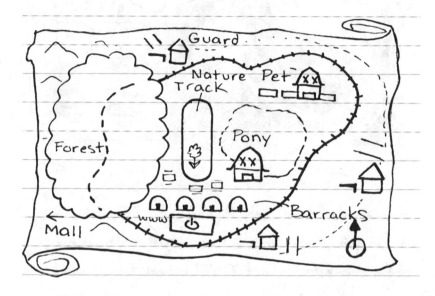

Aside from that, they had pony rides, a farm-style petting zoo, this sappy-looking "safari train" with animatronic wildlife, a "nature walk", which was really an oval track with lots of trees and bushes, and a coffee shop with an internet cafe.

When Janine saw the pony ride area, she went into super-squee mode and could not stop giggling. She kept squealing, "Pony! Pony! Ponieeeee!" Good grief!

Her brain was completely flipped out. I thought she was going to explode into a shower of blueberry muffin crumbs! She was THAT hyper!

Larry was no better. When he saw that mini-train pull up and the conductor dressed like a Native American open the gate, he was all in for that! He made a bee-line for that first seat! I couldn't believe it! Larry is usually so calm and collected, but today, he was bouncing in his seat with a goofy, cheese-eating grin like he'd won the jackpot! Geez, Larry, have some self-respect!

None of those rides did anything for me. The only thing I wanted to do was get into that internet cafe and check the pro-gamer sites for news. Before I could do anything, Mrs. Jefferson squeezed out of her car with Froufrou, who was gasping for air from

being tucked under her owner's big, fat arm. I almost felt sorry for the poor mutt!

I looked up into the sky, hoping to see a meteor with my name on it streak down from the heavens and mercifully put me out of my misery. If only I'd known then what I know now about Woodcreek Mall being so close! If only I'd paid attention to my surroundings instead of gazing down at my navel in utter defeat!

Mrs. Jefferson insisted I take a bag and a pooper-scooper, and walk Froufrou OUTSIDE the campgrounds, where she'd feel more comfortable.

The counselors let me walk Froufrou out there BY MYSELF, with no one watching me!

Eventually, Froufrou did her business and was ready to return to camp. But then, as I pulled her leash to go back, Froufrou started barking. I looked in the direction that made Froufrou nervous, and right there in a tree was a big, mean, nasty-looking vulture!

That sucker was only ten feet away, too! He was just staring at me with a hungry "I'm going to eat you" look! The kind of look that I didn't like one bit! I backed off, but that vulture just stared and didn't move an inch. Froufrou and I made it back okay, but I hope I don't see that thing ever again as long as I live. I wonder, do vultures eat zombies?

I found a few grubs and beetles in some of the trees for supper. I just popped them in my mouth before Froufrou finished her tour. When the Thanksgiving dinner rolled around, I just pretended a fly landed in my food, making me lose my appetite.

By the time the dinner was over, the sun had set, so the camp was lit by the outdoor barbecue pit. The "campfire" inspired Mr. Standish to tell everybody this weird campfire ghost story, "The Tale of Old

Man McFaddle".

At first, it was pretty funny listening to that South Bronx Pilgrim try to scare us with the description of the monster in the woods. He said it had arms nearly twice as long as any human's, with extra-long, clawed, bony fingers that were permanently stained... from blood! Then Mr. Standish talked about the creature's mouth. It was jammed with gnarly teeth that always had bits of decayed brain stuck between them! Normally, anybody would have thought that creature was spooky. But that fake-British/Brooklyn accent of his just made it a joke!

MR. STANDISH MADE HIM SOUND LIKE SOME KIND OF ZOMBIE SHERLOCK HOLMES FROM NEW JERSEY!

"THE TRUTH IS OUT THERE, KIDS!"

Then, Mr. Horshack interrupted and told everybody that what Mr. Standish was describing was actually something called a "cryptid". Something that science has yet to find, but has proof of being real!

I guess it was the far-off look in Mr. Horshack's eyes, or the way his voice kind of quavered while he described the alleged evidence and eyewitness accounts of the brain-eating monster of the woods. I have no idea if Hermit McFaddle is real or not, but Mr. Horshack thinks that he is!

Mrs. Jefferson had to jump in and stop Mr. Horshack's story short because he was definitely

creeping out the kids in the class! Personally, I think
Mr. Horshack watches too much T.V, especially that
FBI Paranormal Files show. But Janine was really
nervous about the woods now, and Larry was shaking
in his camping boots!

Now, every kid in class is spooked out and wide awake
past bedtime here in the camper cabins. Larry is
right here in the bunk under me, and scared out of
his mind that some zombie is going to wander into
camp as soon as he shuts his eyes. The irony is of epic
proportions!

"WH—WHAT ARE YOU WRITING ABOUT IN YOUR JOURNAL, BILL? ZOMBIES?"

"YOU COULD SAY THAT."

There were a lot of ups and downs today. I'm not sure I like it when that happens. Hopefully, operation "Escape Plan" runs smoothly tomorrow...with lots of ups and no downs!

<u>Thursday</u>
Sunny all day.

Today was almost the single worst day of my entire life!

Everything started off pretty nice. All it took was one good look around camp to see that the pony ride and the mini-train ride offered the best views of the surrounding area. The perfect places to scope out the best escape routes. I even checked out a pair of binoculars from the camping supply shack for my "recon mission"!

ZOMBIE KID VISION AT x10 MAGNIFICATION!

The mini-train "recon mission" was first. Larry was in the lead seat with me, which was good, because he made me look less suspicious. I didn't even mind his giddiness as the engineer tooted the horn and yelled "All aboard!" To tell the truth, I was getting into it too. It IS kind of hard not to enjoy yourself on a mini-train ride, you know. Plus, the engineer was a bit of a speed freak. He let the throttle open up on this long straightaway through the forest. Yeah, I admit, it was cool! I almost forgot to use my binoculars to check for escape routes from camp to the road.

Big Harold pointed way up on the hillside to a rickety old shack. He yelled, "Look! Look!! Look!" like he saw a ghost or something. Larry didn't help matters much, either. All he could say was, "It's HIS shack! It's Zombie McFaddle's shack!!!"

I bet Larry was still scared from yesterday night and was ready to jump to conclusions. Eventually, I saw something move up there too. It was a buck deer. I scoped it out through my binoculars, but I was the only one who saw it for what it was. Every other kid on that train swore they saw Zombie McFaddle and not a dumb old buck! Sheesh!

WHY DOES EVERYONE WANT TO POINT UP LIKE THEY SEE SOMETHING WHEN NOBODY REALLY SAW ANYTHING?

The train ride ended, and everyone was still talking about "the sighting." I should've stuck around to try

to get everyone back to their senses, but the pony
rides were starting, and I hurried to get a pony for
the next part of my "recon mission". Janine and
the pony ride lady were there as usual. I understand
the pony ride lady having to stay there—it was
her job. But it was like Janine was duct-taped to
"Butterbun", and that was the way she wanted the
rest of her natural life to be!

"WE HAVE BECOME **ONE!**"

Now that I think about it, getting on that pony was
my only real mistake today. "Princey" did not like
having a zombie kid on his back, not one bit! He must
have smelled me and decided that I was something
that does NOT belong in the saddle. When the pony

ride lady helped me on, she could tell Princey was nervous, but she'd trained her horses to do what she said, and Princey let me on without any more complaints.

The look Princey gave that pony lady was pretty cold, though, like she'd ordered him to carry a scorpion on his back! Then Princey glanced back at me with a different look. I wish I knew then that look meant, "Kid, I'm throwing you off the very minute we get out of my owner's line of sight!"

IT WAS LIKE SAYING "GIDDYUP" TO A 600-LB, FOUR-LEGGED BOTTLE OF CORKED HATE!

We took off for a trail ride through the hills, and I failed to notice at first that Princey started lagging behind the other ponies. I should have known what he was trying to pull, but I was too busy checking for my escape route. As soon as we were out of sight from the pony trainer lady, Princey made his move! He threw me off his saddle so fast, I didn't realize what was happening until I was landing in the bushes!

KER-
BUCK

That pony just trotted himself on up to catch the others, and there was no way I could catch up to a horse. He left me out there to get lost! He probably knew I didn't know the way back! So there I was, trying to get out of those bushes and getting ready to shout for help, when I saw something flying around above the trees.

It was that big, black vulture from yesterday, whom I'd decided to call "Bluto". He hadn't seen me, but if I'd shouted, I'd have given myself away! By the time Bluto was gone, so were the other ponies and their riders. I was all alone in those woods.

About that time, I realized I had skipped breakfast. I was really, really hungry, and there was nothing— and I mean nothing—for me to eat! I wandered around until sundown looking for the right trail back to camp, when I came upon this old, abandoned campground. It was out of repair and completely run down.

I went looking around that creepy old place, hoping to find something to eat, and I found that something, all right. I found HIM—the long-departed Hermit McFaddle! He must have used that old camping area's ranger station for a home and passed away a long time ago. But there was a problem: He smelled good... like beef jerky! I swear, he smelled just like a "Thin Tim"!

MY EYES SAW THE POOR REMAINS OF OLD MAN MCFADDLE...

...BUT MY STOMACH WANTED TO "SNAP INTO A THIN TIM!"

So, I...I took a bite.

I couldn't help it! I took a bite! And oh, it was good! A little crunchy, a little chewy! But just right! I just gnawed on his fingers until there were only 3 left.

Just after I finished snacking, I heard voices. There were people coming into camp! I peeked out the window to see who it was and saw Mr. Standish, Mr. Horshack, and Steve. They were coming my way, led by none other by that rat-fink poodle, Froufrou!

At first I thought about just going out to meet them, but then I noticed the fresh bite marks I'd left on the old hermit's remains. They were obvious! They were still kind of wet, too. I must have slobbered! Then I realized I had a smelly, corpse-eating "mustache" and other smears on my face.

Anyone could have put two and two together and reasoned that someone had just recently eaten from the hermit's body, and that someone was ME! So I hid in the closet. I figured that if I hid and they couldn't find me, everyone would just give up and head back to camp. I could then follow them from a safe distance.

My plan might have worked if not for Froufrou. Man, I cannot stand that dog! She led them right to the door of the ranger station and to the remains of old hermit McFaddle! Steve squealed like a little girl from shining a flashlight on McFaddle's decayed face. I could see everything from a crack in the splintered closet door.

At Steve's yell, Mr. Standish and Mr. Horshack yelled too. But as Mr. Horshack and Steve ran away, Mr. Standish put up his dukes and nervously screamed, "You wanna piece o' me, tough guy? Bring it!!!" He thought he was being tough, but I could see his knees knocking!

"I DON'T SWEAT YOU! I WATCHED ROCKO'S FILMS FOUR HUNDRED AND EIGHTY=T'REE TIMES! NNH!!!"

At first I thought they would just make a break for it, but they settled down after Mr. Standish discovered that it was just an old dead body. But that's also when Mr. Horshack discovered the fresh bite marks on Hermit McFaddle's fingerless hands! Suddenly, Mr. Horshack thought he was some kind of detective who could tell if the bite marks were made by a human mouth.

The evidence pointed to only one thing for him: Those remains were a snack for zombie McFaddle, and they had discovered his nest! Mr. Horshack made Steve film the bite-mark evidence, like he was preparing to reveal to the world the existence of a zombie monster. All he needed to do was open the closet and film me with the stains on my lips to do it!

Right then, at the worst moment possible, my stomach
rumbled! But not just any kind of stomach rumble,
it was a deep, from-the-depths-of-the-Earth
rumble of a hungry little zombie kid! It vibrated the
creaky old floor of that shack and made everybody
stop dead in their tracks! I was so BUSTED! Steve
asked, "What was that?" and Froufrou started to
nervously growl. Slowly, all four of them looked
towards the closet. My hiding place!

That's was when I got an idea. My stomach rumbling
was a sure sign that my guts had brewed up some truly
noxious fumes from the addition of that delicious
beef jerky finger food! I was hoping the gas might be

noxious enough to force everyone to retreat—perhaps even run for their lives! I shifted myself so that my butt was positioned at the peephole and concentrated on ejecting the stinkiest, loudest, most devastating fart I could possibly expel! I had to do it! That fart was my only hope!

TRULY DESPERATE TIMES CALL FOR TRULY DESPERATE MEASURES!

Thankfully, my guts did NOT fail me. The roar from the eruption sounded like a hoarse elephant singing lead vocals for a death metal band on a long, loud note as he gargled molten lava! I swear, I felt the door buckle on its rusty hingles from the shock wave! They probably thought it was thunder in the distance back at Camp Woodchunk!

That was more than enough for Mr. Horshack, Mr. Standish and Steve! They ran out of that shack as fast as they could, bumping and tripping over each other! Froufrou was yelping all the way out of that old abandoned camp area with the rest of that group right behind her! Fortunately, Froufrou's nose was so bent out of shape and her yelps were so loud, I was able to follow those guys back to camp without too much trouble.

Everyone was so weirded out by the racket that Mr. Horshack, Mr. Standish and Steve made that no one even noticed me wandering back into camp. I was able to shower and get into bed while everyone else studied Steve's film evidence at the internet cafe. Larry spotted me sitting on my bunk writing in my journal after all the excitement died down.

"HEY! BILL'S IN THE CAMPER BARRACKS! HE'S BEEN RIGHT HERE THE WHOLE TIME, YOU GUYS!!!"

(GOOD OLD LARRY! HE'S ALWAYS THERE TO TAKE A HINT!)

Larry filled me in later on how Mr. Standish determined that the whole zombie encounter was just with some stinky, sickly, old bear who took up residence in the old ranger station. He talked about how that roar could only have come from a bear with bronchitis, and that he's given medical attention to animals in that condition before. Great. My butt produces bear-like roars. Hopefully, I never have to "roar" again.

The only good thing that came from today's adventures was that I spotted a camp counselor guard station that has a slacker posted on it. I walked right past him into camp, and he never once looked up from his "Twittling" on his ePhone. That station should provide the perfect point of exit when I take Froufrou out for her walk tomorrow.

<u>Friday</u>

Who cares about food and weather at a time like this?

Oh, how I would've loved this next entry to be a play-by-play from the tournament venue floor. Oh, how I wish this was some hype about how I'm all set to destroy the champ and defend our community's honor. But it isn't. I'm writing this from inside a weather-beaten old shack in the middle of the woods, surrounded by a whole army of killer vultures, and it's only a matter of time before they figure out that they can just bust through the only window to get me.

I'd better explain how this all fell apart. The vultures have stopped tearing at the roof, so I can concentrate on what all happened now.

I brought my diary with me in a little side pouch today. I made sure to be seen writing in it so folks wouldn't be suspicious that I had a side pouch...with one of my trusty game controllers in it. It's been in there since I broke its "A" button. I'd forgotten it was even in there until I unpacked my duffel bag on Wednesday night. I would've preferred to have a totally undamaged controller to work with, but I can get the job done with one button unusable. No sweat.

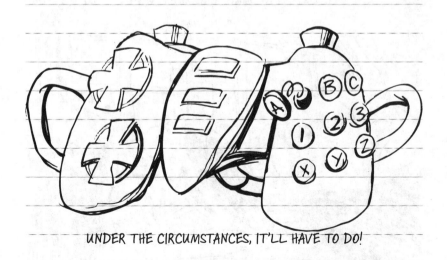

UNDER THE CIRCUMSTANCES, IT'LL HAVE TO DO!

At breakfast, I pretended to eat the ashy-tasting human food as usual. I'd planned to sneak some grub—some real grubs—from this old pine tree I found near the barn. I chatted with Larry for a few minutes like nothing unusual was going on, but I didn't see Janine at all.

BREAKFAST OF
CHAMPION ZOMBIE KIDS!

Everything was going according to my big plan. Everyone was too busy riding ponies and trains and what-not to notice me as I was making my way over to the north guard gate. If only I could have sneaked a little faster, because before I knew it, Steve burst from the boys' barracks, holding his precious digital video camera and yelling, "Who erased my camera's memory card!?!"

He ran around accusing everybody in sight. His entire series was on that flash card, and he never made back-ups! He was red as a beet! I remember thinking how awesome it was that somebody pranked old Steve good! I actually felt a little sorry that it wasn't me, but when Steve, blinded by rage, tripped on that outcropped root near the pony ride and dropped his camera in a pony patty, I couldn't help myself. I LOLed!!!

PONY RIDE

KER-KRP

I LIKE POO

LIFE DOESN'T GET MUCH BETTER THAN THIS!

I laughed out loud until my sides hurt, and that really burned Steve up. It made him so mad that he completely missed sweet, little, pony-riding Janine, the real culprit, giggling her head off at the success of her little prank. Apparently, she'd been plotting revenge since he made her eat those scorpions last week!

An angry Janine is not to be messed with! I have to give her points for that. It was my own fault for not wearing a poker face that the blame got shifted onto me.

Steve sleeps with the camera under his pillow, so how she managed to slip into the boys' barracks unnoticed and delete everything off it is anyone's guess. Then again, she wasn't at breakfast. That was her window of opportunity, I suppose.

CRIME SCENE INVESTIGATOR, OR COUCH-
POTATO SITTING INDOORS—YOU DECIDE

Mr. Horshack was NOT pleased that all that "great
footage" got erased. Thankfully, my fingerprints
were not on the camera. Yes, the vice-principal had
a little fingerprint kit with him! He can analyze
handwriting too! This guy must have been one of
those crime scene investigators before he got the
vice-principal job. Then again, he probably just
learned to do all that stuff after watching too many
cop shows. Mr. Horshack is a slave to network media,
after all.

It was a real treat seeing Steve and Mr. Horshack
try to get fingerprints off a camera that came fresh

out of a pony pie! Luckily, Mr. Horshack insists on gathering evidence before convicting the accused. He might be a jerk in some ways, but he's fair where it counts. Well, he was fair THAT time.

"UH, GUYS? I THINK YOU MISSED A SPOT OVER THERE!"

I guess I was a little too happy that I was cleared, because the very next instant, Mr. Horshack called Mrs. Jefferson over to talk about ME going out on another pooper-scooper run with Froufrou! He must have noticed how me and Froufrou don't exactly "get along" and was having some revenge! If only I'd remembered my poker face, I wouldn't have been in ANY of that mess!

There I was, stuck walking Froufrou. Sure, we were outside the gate, but there was no way I could just take off for the tournament. Not with that poodle in tow! Mrs. Jefferson would come looking for her "Widdle Dickens" within the first thirty minutes of Froufrou's disappearance, and I would've been caught just outside of Woodcreek Mall!

I should have had a better grip on the leash, though, because suddenly Froufrou made a break for it. I had to chase her down, and zombies do not chase things all that well if what they're chasing has a big head start.

"GET BACK HERE!!!"

LE SPRING

"YAP! YAP! YAP!"

So what made Froufrou skedaddle off? Well, she found a dead woodchuck about a quarter of a mile into the woods. I smelled it myself when I got close enough. It smelled like warm buttermilk pancakes and sausage on a cool autumn Sunday morning. I could feel some drool drip out of my mouth too! Those "Thin Tim" fingers didn't tide me over for very long.

I was already hungry again, and that greedy little mutt was chewing all the goodies! You know, I always kind of thought Froufrou was a pickier eater than that. So anyway, I tried to pet her and take some meat for myself, but Froufrou nipped at me and growled! I really hate that dog!

It all fell apart as soon as we turned around to get
back to the camp. Who was staring us right in the
face but "Bluto". That vulture was even bigger
and nastier looking than I remembered. Now he was
staring me down—me AND Froufrou! Then I noticed
he had two of his buddies with him, all perched right
next to each other, flexing those long, razor-sharp
talons of theirs.

They knew—they knew for sure I was a zombie. Fun nature fact: Vultures eat dead things...like zombies. They also snack on slow, yappy little animals for appetizers. We were in deep, dark trouble there, both me and Froufrou. I started to back away, really slow. Then that little nimrod Froufrou took off like a shot, leaving me high and dry for the vultures to eat!

Bluto started flapping and came right for me. Luckily, I can dodge really well when I want to. I could stop one or two from grabbing me, but not three! So I shouted really loud for help and for them to leave me alone! I knew I probably wasn't close enough to camp for anyone to hear me over the petting zoo and ponies and everything, but at least it startled the vultures.

They took off, but before I could make a break for it, I looked over my shoulder and saw Froufrou. She'd gotten herself caught in an old rabbit snare! Served her right!

KARMA DON'T PLAY!

I should have left that crying and yelping traitor for the vultures to buy me some extra time, but I just couldn't bring myself do it. The trap was a wire snare that was set really tight. There was no way out for her, and I didn't have anything to slice the wire. Then I remembered the trick Mom used to cut my fingernails. I got real close and I BIT right through that wire. My teeth worked better than any wire cutters I've ever used! I wonder what else I can bite through with these chompers?

I WOULDN'T BE SURPRISED AT ALL IF I COULD DO THIS!

What did the mutt do in gratitude after I saved her hide? She took off AGAIN! Just in time for two more vultures to join the party! They start circling and taking turns diving at me! With my zombie running speed, there was no chance I could get away, either! But I saw this shack way up on the hill—the same shack big Harold spotted yesterday—and I hustled up there as fast as my lead zombie feet could carry me!

I just barely made it inside and closed the door! But now I'm trapped. More vultures have been showing up, too.

And now they've started pecking at the window...

Saturday

Too happy to be alive—uh, in one piece to worry about food and weather.

Those vultures broke through, but guess what? Mr. Standish and the camp councilor cavalry were able to scare away the vultures and come to my rescue in the nick of time! And you'll never guess how they found me—Froufrou! That little stinker ran away to go for some help! Son of a gun!

After that, I wasn't even mad that I'd missed the tournament. I was just glad to get out of that shack in one piece! I guess it takes something like that for you to realize that things aren't as bad as they could be.

EATEN BY VULTURES

MISSING TOURNEY

STUBBING MY TOE

SOMETIMES, YOU HAVE TO PUT THINGS INTO PERSPECTIVE.

By the time I was safely back at camp, it was evening. But what was weird was that the power was out. The blackout lasted all evening, so we just sat around listening to more of Mr. Standish's campfire stories. I sat through a whole story before I realized Froufrou was right there and I was petting her. I guess she's not that bad a dog, after all. It IS still a shame I missed out on the tournament, though. Oh, well.

<u>Monday</u>
Rainy all day.
Homemade rancid buttermilk road waffles—mmm!

Sorry I haven't written in this for a while. A ton of
stuff happened.

Once I lost my shot at the Japanese champ, I stopped
obsessing over it and just relaxed at Camp Woodchunk.
The place was actually pretty neat, and the time
just whizzed on by. I didn't even mind having to
walk Froufrou after every meal. We stayed clear of
vultures, though.

And get this: The power stayed off the whole weekend and didn't come back on until we left on Sunday night! I found out what happened after I got online at home. The power went out for that whole grid on Friday when some giant birds tried to perch on the power lines near Camp Woodchunk. They broke the power cables with their weight! I know who those birds were! I hope they got shocked!

BUZZERDS

Here's the real kicker, though: Woodcreek Mall is on the same power grid. The tournament got canceled before the first match even started! They've rescheduled the tournament for this coming Friday afternoon! The champ is still going to be there, too. I still get my chance to defend our gaming community's honor after all! I felt like the biggest bully of all time had just played the biggest practical joke of all time on me! I guess that's just life?

"AWW! DON'T BE MAD! I WAS JUST FOOLIN' WITH YA!"

"C-CUT IT OUT!!!"

No practice today, though. I'm going to go walk Froufrou for Mrs. Jefferson on my way to Larry's. Janine's going to be there too. She's got the memory card she copied from Steve's now-empty video camera. It seems Steve got some pretty good shots of the ponies and the train besides being a jerk for his stupid show, so we're going to edit it together and make a private viewing of our own show: *Bug Bites and Camp Sights!*

Bonus Round! (Dadadada da daaaaa!!!)

You know, there's one thing I've been forgetting to jot down here. It's something I've been looking into for months, but I've never had the chance to really go into it.

THE ZOMBIE VIRUS

MOM BROUGHT HOME FOR DINNER!

ZOMBIE & MAC CHEEZ

You see, Mom wasn't always all slouchy and stiff. Last year, she was the star pupil of her Pilates class! When I was little, I used to put Bricko blocks on her forehead as she did sit-ups just to see them launched into the air! And when I was in kindergarten, she used to tow my training wheel bike when she jogged!

So when middle school started, Mom was pretty still
pretty zippy! But that's also when her new "job"
as a medicine test volunteer for a various companies
began. And here's the thing: Mom didn't just volunteer
for one company after another. She signed on to
volunteer with like three or four of them at the same
time! She'd spend two hours every day with the testing
staff of each of those company. By the end of that
week, she had a bunch of huge paychecks to cash! I
spotted the check stubs on the coffee table. She made
more in a month than Dad did in half a year!

So here's my theory: If one of those companies
injected Mom with the virus, they would probably
realize what they had and they would know that Mom

was now a zombie. But if Mom's zombieness came from a strange combination of all the test chemicals and all those nonfat, soy lattes she's got in her system...all that would have been needed was a jolt of static electricity from the doorknob, and boom!

ZOM BREW

That very same night I became a zombie was the last night Mom cooked up a normal-looking meal for me. By then, she was a plague-bearing playground, and some of her newly evolved zombie germs made it into my big ol' bowl of mac and cheese! Ugh! I knew I should have put on some hot sauce!

But then, with my luck, the hot-sauced zombie bacteria would have given me super-heated nuclear zombie gas powers instead of my normal nuclear zombie gas powers! Just like some of those radioactive superheroes cursing their inconvenient transformations, it's still possible to look back at the accident that changed me and think, "Well, it could have been worse..."

*"DON'T MAKE ME GASSY.
YOU WOULDN'T LIKE ME
WHEN I'M GASSY!"*

Anyway, back to the mac and cheese. It tasted funny, like styrofoam dipped in plastic cheese oil. At the first bite, I just thought it was maybe a bad noodle or three pushing all the tasty ones out of the way to do a stale, bitter elbow drop on my tastebuds. By the third bite, I was beginning to think that Mom was messing with me or something!

GRAW   GRAAW

NOODLES OF THE LIVING DEAD!

I thought she was feeding me some of her weird, homemade whoda-howda-whadda-heck-IS-this noodles instead of the store-brought dinners I used to ask for. So, I took a few more bites, just be be sure. But by the time I was on bite number seven, I could feel my toes going a little numb, and I decided something was amiss! I didn't even eat all of it, but I guess by then, the noodles I'd already devoured contained just enough zombie cheese to begin transforming my biology!

So Mom totally cleaned off her plate, and after she went to lie down, I dumped my leftovers right into the trash. Then, to cover my tracks—I didn't want Mom to see a pile of noodles in the garbage pail—I volunteered to take the trash out to the dumpster. Just the place for some ordinary house cats to climb inside and have a snack!

So there you have it—my theory of zombie relativity! Something from Mom's old medical testing job, mixed with something else from Mom's old medical testing job or—OR with the soy lattes, which completely worked their caffeinated ways into Mom's system to create a colony of mutated germs that have modified our human genes!

But are we still contagious? I haven't seen anyone else change into a zombie. Maybe you have to eat the zombie germs to get changed. Getting bitten's the classic method—maybe it spreads that way. I don't know. But I do know that being in class with a zombie, being on a school bus with a zombie, and/or having to smell zombie gas doesn't change you. That is...I don't think it does.

I guess we'll just have to wait and see.

NEXT TIME

ZOMBIE KID DIARIES

WALKING DAD